PiPER REED

THe GREaT GyPSy

KIMBERLY WILLIS HOLT

PiPER REED
THE GREAT GYPSY

Illustrated by
CHRISTINE DAVENIER

SQUARE
FISH

HENRY HOLT AND COMPANY
NEW YORK

SQUARE
FISH

An Imprint of Macmillan

PIPER REED, THE GREAT GYPSY. Text copyright © 2008 by Kimberly Willis Holt.
Illustrations copyright © 2008 by Christine Davenier. All rights reserved. Printed in May 2009 in the
United States of America by R.R. Donnelley & Sons Company, Harrisonburg, Virginia.
For information, address Square Fish, 175 Fifth Avenue, New York, NY 10010.

Square Fish and the Square Fish logo are trademarks of Macmillan and are used by
Henry Holt and Company under license from Macmillan.

Library of Congress Cataloging-in-Publication Data
Holt, Kimberly Willis.
Piper Reed, the great gypsy / Kimberly Willis Holt ; illustrated by Christine Davenier.
p. cm.
Summary: While her father, a Navy Chief, is on ship duty for six months,
nine-year-old Piper stays busy with new neighbors,
Christmas at a spaceship beach house, a trip to New Orleans,
and especially the upcoming Gypsy Club pet show.
ISBN: 978-0-312-56136-9
[1. Family life—Florida—Fiction. 2. Sisters—Fiction. 3. Pet shows—Fiction. 4. Schools—Fiction.
5. United States. Navy—Fiction. 6. Pensacola (Fla.)—Fiction.] I. Davenier, Christine, ill. II. Title.
PZ7.H74023Pit 2008 [Fic]—dc22 2007046941

Originally published in the United States by Henry Holt and Company
Square Fish logo designed by Filomena Tuosto
First Square Fish Edition: 2009
10 9 8 7 6 5 4 3 2 1
www.squarefishbooks.com

To my dad, Ray Willis,
who gave twenty-one years
to the United States Navy—
Thank you, "Chief."

—K. W. H.

CONTENTS

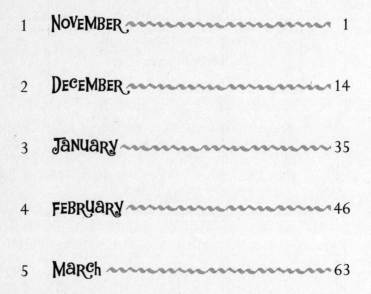

1

NOVEMBER

My little sister, Sam, knelt on the sofa, staring out the window. Our next-door neighbors moved off base last week, and she was watching for our new neighbors to arrive.

That's the way the Navy life was. Someone was always coming and someone was always going. Before we moved to Pensacola, we'd lived in California, Texas, Guam, Mississippi, and New Hampshire. Just when a place started to feel like home, we had to leave, again.

"The moving van is here!" Sam called out.

Tori and I rushed over to the window. My older sister was twelve and boy crazy. She probably wanted some goofy guy to move next door so that she could flutter her eyelashes at him. I was hoping for a fourth-grader, another potential Gypsy Club member. I started the Gypsy Club when we lived in San Diego. I'd already recruited three members while in Pensacola.

"I hope there's a five-year-old girl, just like me, moving in," said Sam. She leaned to the far right, stretching her neck as if she expected a kindergartner to pop out of the van.

I pointed to Sam's reflection in the window. "There she is."

"Where?"

"Right there. She looks exactly like you."

When Sam caught on, she stuck out her chin. "I'm not stupid."

"I know. You're a prodigy—a spelling bee prodigy."

Tori gave me a shove with her elbow. "Move over, Piper. You're hogging all the space, and I can't see."

"You just take up more room," I told her. When I wanted to get back at Tori, I mentioned her chubby body.

Tori's face turned purple. "You're mean, Piper Reed!"

She was right. Since Chief left, I'd said something mean every day. That meant I'd said seven mean things because seven days had passed since our dad left for ship duty.

A big calendar hung on our kitchen wall with a red X crossed through each day. Chief would be gone six long months. Each day we took turns marking off another day. Even Mom got a turn. In the Reed household we took turns for everything. And that means I'm

always in the middle because *I am* the middle.

Mom handed the marker to me. "Go ahead, Piper. It's your turn."

"Why do I always have to be last?" Sam asked as I marked an X over November 11. I guess there were worse things than being in the middle. At least I wasn't Sam who would always be the baby of the family, even when she was ninety-five years old.

"It can be fun to be last," Tori told Sam. "Haven't you heard 'Save the best for last'?"

"That's easy for you to say," I said. "You're always first."

Sam fixed her hands on her hips. "Well, I'm going to be the first one to kiss Daddy when he gets off the ship."

Mom sighed, but she wasn't paying any attention to us. She stood at the kitchen table, looking over her paint box. Monday she'd start teaching art at our school. That's when our art teacher, Mrs. Kimmel, goes on maternity leave. School would be weird having Mom there. I hoped she wouldn't ask me in front of the class if I remembered to brush my teeth.

"What about papier-mâché?" Mom asked, thumbing through newspaper scraps.

"We did papier-mâché piggy banks last week," I said. "Remember?"

Mom made a snapping noise with her tongue. "Oh, yeah. Drats!"

"Why can't they do papier-mâché again?" Tori asked.

"I want the students to make something different."

"You could let us have recess during art," I suggested.

Tori scowled. "Why would she do that?"

I shrugged. "Well, that would be different."

"We didn't do papier-mâché," said Sam.

"You didn't?" Mom sounded excited.

"Mom," I said, "think about it. Twenty kindergartners with a bunch of mush and newspaper strips? They would be a disaster."

"Oh," she said. "Good point."

Sam looked offended. "No, we won't."

"Piper is right," Mom said.

Sam frowned at me. "You spoil everything!"

"Sam, you could handle it," said Mom, "but so many of your other classmates wouldn't be able to create papier-mâché without making a huge mess."

Sam straightened her back. "That's true."

Great, I thought. Sam, the prodigy. Sam, who could read better than me, and now I couldn't even count on her to make a big mess with papier-mâché.

Mom turned off the pot of beans on the stove. They'd been cooking all day, and the smell of sausage and onions filled our kitchen.

Grabbing her sketchbook, Mom said, "We'll eat dinner soon, but first I'm going to take a bath. Creative ideas always come to me in the tub."

"Like a think tank?" Sam asked.

Mom smiled. "Yes, I guess you could say that."

Maybe I'd take a long soak later because I

needed a good idea, too. I wanted to accomplish something fantastic so Chief would be extra proud of me when he returned.

I walked over to the computer. "I'll check our e-mail to see if Chief wrote to us yet."

Tori and Sam followed me.

Every day Chief e-mailed us. Sometimes there was a message waiting in the morning. Sometimes it was there after school. But no matter what, a message was there every day. We could count on it.

> *Dear Girls,*
>
> *I've only been gone a week and already it feels like a year. But that's because it's the first week. The time will pass quickly, just wait and see. But don't grow too much. I won't recognize you.*
>
> *By the way, I forgot to tell you a few things. Make sure you print the attachment and put it on the refrigerator.*

That could mean only one thing. We opened the attachment.

"Great," Tori muttered when a list appeared.

1. *Sweep the porch every afternoon.*
2. *Rake the yard once a month.*
3. *Wash the car at least every other Saturday. Don't forget the tire rims.*

Chief didn't need a think tank to make lists. He could make one anytime—while he ate a Big Mac or watched TV or stretched out on the couch. Mom called it his hobby, but I think it's because you have to know how to make lists when you're a chief in the U.S. Navy.

A few minutes later, Sam called out, "They're here! The new neighbors are here!"

The three of us raced outside. I decided I wouldn't mind if there was a bratty girl Sam's age or a goofy boy Tori's age, as long as there was someone my age. Someone who could become an official Gypsy Club member and say "Get off the bus!" when they were excited. It was my goal to spread that saying around the world, and I'd already spread it to California and Florida.

A blue car had parked next door. A second later, a man got out from behind the driver's seat and then his wife opened the passenger door. The lady smiled at us.

I wasn't sure of their rank, but I saluted

them anyway. "Hi. Welcome to NAS Pensacola, home of the Blue Angels!"

The man's face broke out into a big grin. He even had dimples.

Tori elbowed me. "What are you? The welcome committee?"

"That's a lovely welcome," the lady said. "My name is Yolanda and this is Abe."

"Good to meet you," Abe said. "I guess the people in Florida are as warm as the climate."

They seemed nice, but where were their kids? Maybe their kids were grown. But Yolanda and Abe looked too young for that. Maybe they didn't have any kids. My shoulders sank.

Then Yolanda opened the car's back door and ducked her head inside. I heard her say, "Come on, Brady. Don't be shy."

Brady? That could be a girl or a boy. That could be a five-year-old, or a twelve-year-old, or maybe a nine-year-old. That could be a future Gypsy Club member.

But a moment later Yolanda straightened and in her arms was a little kid. A *big* little kid. Almost the same size as Sam.

Yolanda kissed the top of his head. "This is Brady. He's two years old. He's kind of tall for his age."

Brady held out three fingers. "Twee!" he said.

"You have a good ways to go before you're three," Yolanda said, smiling.

We stood there, studying Brady. He had dimples just like Abe. None of us said a word. Then Bruna walked over to them and wagged her tail.

Brady pointed to her, bouncing on his mother's hip. "Dog!" he said.

Great, I thought. Just what I need—another child prodigy!

2

December

"Christmas won't be Christmas without Daddy," Sam said at breakfast.

Christmas was a week away and Chief had been gone more than a month.

"No, it won't," Mom said. "So we'll have to make sure it's good and different."

I stopped blowing bubbles in my chocolate milk with my straw. "What do you mean?"

"I have a surprise." Mom beat the eggs and milk together for French toast. Some of the egg mixture spilled on the floor, causing a puddle. Mom hadn't noticed yet, but Bruna had. She was licking it up at a great speed. Who needed a mop when we had Super Poodle?

"Can you give us a hint?" I asked. I was the best guesser in the family. I could be a detective if I didn't want to be a Navy pilot and fly for the Blue Angels.

"One hint?" Mom stared at the ceiling. "Hmm. Should I give a tiny hint?"

"Please," we begged.

"Okay," Mom said. "But only one. Ready?"

"Yes!" we shouted.

"You have to pack your bags."

"That means the surprise is off-base," I said.

Mom winked. "Exactly, Gypsy Girl."

That night Sam whispered to me from her bed across the room. "I think I know where we're going."

"Where?" I asked.

"The Audubon Aquarium of the Americas."

"In New Orleans? Why do you think that?"

Sam sighed as if I was the stupidest person on the base. "Because Mommy knows how much I like fish."

"Just because you have a goldfish named Peaches doesn't mean we're going to the aquarium."

"We'll see."

"Yeah," I said. "We'll see."

"Hmph!"

It was dark but I knew Sam was crossing her arms over her chest. She did that every time she thought she was right about something. Even if she was dead wrong!

Then I added, "But I'm sure *I* know where we're going."

Sam kept quiet, so I did too. I wasn't going to say a word until she begged.

Silence.

I bit my tongue so hard it throbbed.

Finally Sam released a long, dramatic sigh. "Okay, I give up. Tell me."

"Nah," I said. "I wouldn't want to ruin the surprise."

"I can still be surprised."

"Nah. It would spoil all the fun."

"No, it wouldn't," Sam said.

"Welllll . . ."

"It won't." Now her voice sounded squeaky like she was about to cry. "I promise," she begged. "I can still be surprised. I promise."

"Okay." Then very slowly, I sounded out each word. "I . . . think . . . we're . . . going . . . to . . . Disney World."

"Ooooo," Sam squealed. Her heels made soft thumps against the mattress.

"Shhh! Tori might hear." The vent between our rooms kept us from having secrets.

"Disney World," Sam whispered. "I love Disney World."

"We've never been," I said.

"I know. But I love it anyway."

The day before Christmas Eve, Mom said, "Okay, Gypsy Girls, pack your bags for three days. And don't forget your toothbrush, Piper."

She never forgot that I had four cavities. It didn't help that Tori had none and was three years older. And of course Sam brushed hers forever just to make me look bad. When we got inside the car, I was excited. We even got to take Bruna. Of course, that meant Sam got to bring Peaches. She carried her in a plastic sandwich bag with some water while she held Annie, her doll, in the other hand. The fishbowl was packed in a box with some towels in the back of the van.

"Can we wear blindfolds?" I asked.

"Sure," Mom said.

"Get off the bus!" I hollered.

"Do we have to wear blindfolds?" Tori asked.

Mom smiled. "No, not unless you want to."

"I'm busy writing anyway," Tori said, then she scribbled something in her poetry notebook.

She didn't fool me. She liked surprises, too. As long as they didn't mess up her hair.

Sam and I tied scarves around our eyes. I already figured out we weren't going to Disney World. Orlando was too far away to stay blindfolded the entire trip.

I could tell we were still on base because Mom drove as slow as an ant crawling across

a picnic blanket, carrying a crumb on its back.

"I'll bet we're passing the park," I said.

"Correct," said Tori.

A few seconds later, Sam said, "I'll bet we're passing the chapel right now."

"Yep," Tori said.

And then when Mom accelerated, I shouted, "We just left the base."

But this time, Tori didn't say anything.

"Well?" I asked.

"I'm bored with that game. If you want to know, look yourself."

"I'm not peeking."

"Neither am I," said Sam.

Less than thirty minutes later, Mom said, "We're almost there."

"I can't wait," Sam squealed.

Finally Mom stopped the car. "Okay, we're here!" she announced.

I yanked off my blindfold. In front of us, before our very eyes, was the spaceship beach house that I discovered with Chief, the week

before he left. It was as if Martians had landed on Pensacola Beach. The round white house was built high off the ground. An alien stared out the window in our direction, waving.

"Get off the bus!" I yelled.

"Wow!" Sam said. "Is that a *real* alien?"

Tori clucked her tongue. "Of course not. It's made out of paper." Her voice sounded flat. I could tell she was disappointed at Mom's surprise. She probably had hoped we were going to the Mall of America. Ever since she heard about the mall with hundreds of stores and a water park inside, she'd begged Chief to take a vacation there. The water park sounded fun, but I hated to shop.

"Come on, Tori," Mom said. "We'll have a good time. Look how close we are to the beach."

Tori stared out at the shoreline. "It's too cold to sunbathe."

"Did we buy the house?" I asked.

Mom chuckled. "No. I rented it for three nights. I got a super deal on it. Seems most people don't like to stay at the beach during the winter."

"Gee, I wonder why," Tori muttered.

We had to climb a tall flight of steps to get to the circular house. I carried Bruna up. From the top step there was a great view of the gulf. Listening to the water splash against the shore, I took a deep breath. The salty air tickled my nose.

What was inside? Spaceship seats? Maybe a floating bed?

But when Mom opened the door, it looked like a room in any other house, with a brown tweed couch, an orange recliner, and a glass coffee table.

My heart sank.

Sam headed toward a bedroom. A second

later, I heard her say, "I'm floating! Floating, floating!"

Tori and I rushed to the bedroom to discover Sam sitting in the middle of a bed, wobbling back and forth.

"Oh." Tori rolled her eyes. "It's just a water bed."

"Yay!" I hurried and plopped next to Sam, riding the waves. "This isn't a water bed! This is a spaceship bed. A bed that will travel through the Milky Way and take us to other galaxies. Beam me up, Scotty!"

"Yeah, beam me up, Scotty," Sam said. Then she wrinkled her forehead. "Who's Scotty?"

"You know, the guy on those *Star Trek* shows."

Sam searched the rest of the house, running from room to room. "Where's the Christmas tree?" she asked.

"Oh, no." Mom grimaced. "I guess I didn't think of everything."

"Maybe we can find a tree lot," Tori suggested, a bit cheerfully.

"Yeah," I said. "We passed one before we drove over the bridge."

Tori stretched out her arm and pointed at me. "I knew it. You peeked."

"So what?" I said. "Mom didn't say we couldn't look."

Mom straightened. "Girls, that's a super idea. Let's check out that tree lot after we unpack."

Mom put the food in the fridge and cabinets, then we got back in the car. Soon we came to the Christmas-tree lot. A sign posted in front read FIFTY PERCENT OFF!

There were four trees left and only one was really decent. It was taller than Mom.

I plucked a needle from a branch.

Grabbing the tree's trunk, Mom said, "Well, I guess this will have to be it. Tori, take hold of the top part."

Then I noticed the tree next to it. The scrawny evergreen was only as tall as Sam. A few of the branches leaned to the right.

Some had hardly any needles. It was perfect.

Mom and Tori headed toward the salesman, but I stopped them.

"Wait, Mom."

"Yes?"

"You said this was going to be a really *different* Christmas, right?"

Mom wrinkled her forehead. "Right."

"Then shouldn't we get a *different* Christmas tree?"

"Well, sure." She studied the tree she and Tori held.

I wrapped my fingers around the trunk of the little tree. "Let's get the saddest one."

"This is ridiculous," Tori said. "Even the tree is going to be lousy."

I was bound to lose the battle, but then Sam surprised me and said, "Yeah, let's get the saddest tree and make it happy."

"A Charlie Brown tree," I said.

Mom eased down the trunk of the pretty tree. "That would be different."

Tori's eyes bulged like they were going to pop out of their sockets. Usually that meant she was about to yell. But she just glared at me, turning three shades of purple.

The man charged Mom only five dollars for the tree. Then he threw in a tree stand.

"What the heck?" he said. "It's Christmas. Besides, no one else would have bought that tree."

"Gee, I wonder why," Tori muttered. The purple was gone from her face. Now her cheeks just looked like they had a bad sunburn.

Back at the spaceship, the sun had disappeared and the sky had started to get dark. We ate dinner, then decided to make ornaments for the tree. Mom took out some of her paints and gave us paper from the sketch pad. She placed scissors and glue on the table. We drank hot chocolate while we drew aliens, planets, and spaceships. Then we strung popcorn together with a needle and thread.

We hung our ornaments on the tree, listening to a Chipmunks Christmas CD the owners had left in the player. After we finished, we stood back and admired our work. Something was missing though. Chief! Every year he lifted Sam up, and she put an angel at the top of the tree.

"We need an angel," I said. "I'll make one."

Sam watched over my shoulder as I drew. "Make her dress pink," she ordered. "And give her a crown."

"Angels don't wear crowns," I said. "They have halos."

"But this angel is smart, so she has a crown." Sam was referring to *her* crown, the one she received when she won the spelling bee at our school in San Diego. She used to wear it everywhere until we moved to Pensacola. She got teased on our first day at school. I guess this was a sign that she wasn't ready to give it up entirely.

Maybe it was easier to have dyslexia, like me, than to be super smart, like Sam and Tori. I didn't get worked up about wearing crowns, winning spelling bees, or making straight A's. Once Tori cried because she got a B-minus on a paper. Mom and Chief are excited when I get a B-minus.

After I finished coloring the angel, Tori taped a paper cone to the back. Then Sam fit the angel on the top branch. The branch leaned so far to the right that the angel looked like it was doing a back dive. No one said anything though, because Sam looked so happy.

The next day was Christmas Eve. If it were summer, we could swim, but now it was cool outside.

"That doesn't mean we can't play on the beach," Mom said.

Tori took a picture of the sand castle we built. It was just a puny castle though. One day I was going to design a big one. It would be so magnificent that people would call me a champion castle designer. Maybe they would even call me a prodigy.

Later, Mom joined us, and we lay down on the sand, moving our legs and arms like we did in the snow on our Colorado vacation a couple of years ago. Bruna pranced around us, barking. She must have wanted us to get up. When we did, we looked at the four angels we'd made, Mom's tall one next to the three of ours. Bruna's paw prints were all around the figures.

"Look," I said. "Snowflakes! I mean *sand-flakes*!"

But there should have been five angels.

"Quick, Tori," I said, "take a picture before the tide washes them away. We can send it to Chief. Then he'll be a part of our day. A part of our Christmas."

"Great idea, Piper," Mom said.

Before going to bed that night, I took out my sketchbook and started drawing my dream castle. My castle had a couple of towers and a moat. It was truly amazing.

Before long, Mom announced, "Twenty-two hundred! Lights out!"

It was funny to hear Mom use military time. She'd only started doing that since Chief had left.

Every Christmas Eve, I tossed and turned in my bed. But tonight I wasn't thinking about presents. I was still trying to come up with something spectacular that would make Chief extra proud of me. Bruna curled in a tight ball next to my belly. That's when my fantastic idea came to me. The Gypsy Club could have a dog show. I would teach Bruna amazing tricks and we would win. When I finally fell asleep, I dreamed that I held a giant trophy. Bruna and I were standing in front of a huge sand castle with two towers and a moat.

Christmas day we opened our presents. I got my very own easel with paints and paintbrushes. Later we had an early dinner. It was only turkey, mashed potatoes, and sweet peas, but we called the dishes Moon Gobbler, Milky Way Mush, and Alien Eyeballs.

Mom was right. We'd really had a different Christmas. And it was pretty good after all. But the best part of the day was when we returned home and checked our e-mail. We had a message from each set of grandparents and one from Chief. Without hesitating, we opened Chief's first. It started out, "Merry Christmas, my Gypsy Girls. Welcome back to Earth!"

3

JANUARY

Michael and Nicole sat across from Hailey and me. We were eating the snicker doodle cookies that Mom and Sam baked in the morning. Our home still smelled of cinnamon.

I knocked on the coffee table with my fist. "I call the first Gypsy Club meeting of the new year to order."

"I second that," Michael said through a mouthful of cookie.

"Okay," I said. "Then we can begin."

Nicole cleared her throat. "Er . . . um. Excuse me."

"Yes?" I asked.

"You didn't ask for the nays."

"Oh, brother," Michael groaned. "We need another guy in this club."

"You have to ask if anyone is opposed," Nicole said.

"Opposed to what?" I asked.

"Starting the meeting," she said.

I shrugged my shoulders. "Any opposed?"

Nicole raised her finger. "I might be."

Hailey sighed and leaned against the couch.

"Why?" Michael snapped. "Why are you opposed?"

Nicole blinked. "I didn't say I *was* opposed. I said I might be."

"Well?" I said, waiting.

Nicole ran her tongue over her braces, then announced, "I'm not."

Hailey frowned. "You're not what?"

"Opposed," said Nicole.

Michael shook his head. "Oh, brother. It's hard to believe we're twins. I bet they got the babies mixed up at the hospital. I bet my real twin is walking around with someone who looks like Nicole. And he's saying, Why me?"

Nicole had a blank look on her face. I guess she was used to Michael wishing aloud that he wasn't her brother. We stood, saluted, and recited the Gypsy Club creed.

> We are the Gypsies of land and sea.
> We move from port to port.
> We make friends everywhere we go.
> And everywhere we go, we let people know
> That we're the Gypsies of land and sea.

"Let's get down to business," I said. "I think we should have a dog show in the summer. Maybe July. That will give us a few months to teach our dogs some tricks." Plus Chief would be home in May, in time to see Bruna and me win. Nicole and Michael's mom, Ms. Austin, served on the same ship as Chief. That meant she would be home in time to see me win, too.

"I don't have a dog," Nicole said.

We'd only lived here a couple of months. I didn't know what pets my new friends owned. I guess I'd thought everyone had a dog.

Nicole pulled her sleeve over her wrist. "I'm allergic to dogs. I have a cat though. Can I put my cat in the show?"

"Yeah," Michael said. "I have a guinea pig. I want a dog, but I can't have one because Nicole's allergic to them. She's allergic to everything. Anyway, my guinea pig already knows how to do a couple of tricks."

I thought about it a second. "Well, cats and guinea pigs can't be in a dog show."

"I have a dog," Hailey said.

"How about a pet show?" Michael asked. "Then it can be any kind of pet."

I nodded. "Okay." After all, Bruna was going to win anyway. I'd have to train her, but she already knew how to do half a trick. When I threw a ball, she fetched it. She just needed to learn the bringing it back part.

All of a sudden, Sam popped up from behind the couch. She was always spying on us. "Yay! That means Peaches can be in the pet show, too."

"Peaches is a fish," I said.

Sam squeezed between Nicole and me. "So? I'm going to teach her some tricks."

"You're not even in the Gypsy Club," I snapped.

"Yeah," Michael piped in. "You're not in our club, pip-squeak."

I frowned at Michael. "Hey, don't call my sister pip-squeak."

"Well, she's not old enough to be in the Gypsy Club," said Hailey. Then she grabbed the last cookie.

Sam's eyes widened. "But I'm a prodigy."

I rose up on my knees so that I could look down on Michael and Hailey. After all, I was in charge. I started the Gypsy Club. That should count for something.

"Who said you had to be a Gypsy Club member to be in the Gypsy Club pet show?" I could hardly believe what was coming out of my mouth. A minute earlier I hadn't wanted Sam to be in the pet show either. But I didn't like anyone bossing my sister around. (Except me.)

Nicole knelt so that she was even with me. "I don't see anything wrong with Sam being in the pet show."

"Well," Hailey began, "since she's not a member, she'll have to pay an entrance fee."

"How much?" Sam asked.

Michael and Hailey huddled their heads together. It didn't seem fair that they were discussing the fee without Nicole and me, but I let them because I knew what would happen no matter what price they decided on.

"Three dollars!" they called out.

Sam skipped off toward her bedroom.

Michael stretched out his arms, locked his fingers together, and cracked his knuckles. "There. That will keep her out."

Too bad Michael didn't know about Sam's piggy bank. She saved her money better than Tori and I did. When we got birthday money from our grandparents, Tori and I spent it the day it arrived. Not Sam. The money she received for her first birthday was still stuffed in that pig. Grandpa Reed teased her that she was saving money in her piggy bank so she could live high off the hog one day.

A moment later, Sam returned with her piggy bank. She flipped it over, pulled the rubber plug, and shook out the money. Crumpled dollar bills, quarters, nickels, dimes, and pennies landed on the carpet. Michael's and Hailey's eyes grew wide.

Nicole leaned toward the pile of money. "Wow, you're rich!"

Sam gathered the bills, smoothing out each dollar, stacking them in a crisp pile. Then she turned to the coins. "I'm going to pay with pennies."

She began to count, "One, two, three . . ."

Michael moaned and sank back against the couch.

A long minute later, Sam was still counting. "Forty-eight, forty-nine . . ."

"Okay, okay," Hailey said. "So you've got three dollars."

"I'm not finished yet," Sam said. "Fifty, fifty-one . . ." When Sam reached three hundred, she pointed to the pile of tarnished pennies. "That's three dollars!"

I stood and held out my hand to her. "Terrific! Welcome to the Gypsy Club pet show!"

Sam jumped to her feet and shook my hand. "Does this mean I'm in the Gypsy Club?"

"Don't push your luck," I told her. I tapped my fist on the coffee table. "Meeting adjourned." Then I stared at Nicole. "Unless anyone is opposed."

4

FEBRUARY

Every day after school, I trained Bruna. I threw the ball. She ran after it, picked up the ball, and took off running around the yard.

Then, just as I'd seen a dog trainer do on TV, I raised my right arm straight up. With a commanding voice, I ordered, "Come here, Bruna!" Then I let my arm fall to my side.

Bruna just circled faster with the ball locked between her teeth.

At dinner one night, Tori asked, "Why don't

you try giving her treats? Pets usually like to be rewarded."

Sam's eyes widened. "That's a great idea!"

I wasn't so sure. But the next day I took two dog biscuits with me in the backyard.

Next door, Brady was playing in his sandbox. "Hi, Piper!"

"Hi, Brady!"

Then he called out, "Hi, Boona!"

Bruna wagged her tail.

"I'm twee!"

"Not yet," I reminded him.

Tori came outside and plopped on a lawn chair with a book. She wore her big white-framed sunglasses just like the pair she'd seen her favorite movie star, Margie Marcel, wear in some fashion magazine. The lenses were so dark, I couldn't see Tori's eyes, but I knew she was spying on me, waiting for me to make a fool of myself.

I showed Bruna the biscuits. "See, Bruna. See the treat?"

Bruna wagged her tail. When I threw the ball, Bruna stayed put, staring at the biscuit in my other hand. Then she stood on all fours and barked.

I pointed to the ball and jumped in place. "Fetch! Get the ball! Then you can have a biscuit."

Bruna barked. I waited. She barked again. Finally I just gave her the biscuit. Maybe if she knew how good it tasted, she'd want to earn the other one.

But when I threw the ball again and hollered, "Fetch!" she wagged her tail and barked. I surrendered and gave her the other biscuit.

Tori peered over the book. "Good girl, Bruna. You taught Piper a trick!"

The next day, Mom asked us to help her take some plastic crates out to the car. They were filled with scraps of magazine pictures, wrapping paper, and plastic containers of glitter. One crate held a bunch of empty tissue boxes.

"We're going to make memory boxes," Mom said.

On the way to school, Mom talked about how she came up with her idea. "First I was going to have the students make Valentine cards, but everyone's done that before. So I started thinking about how the students could make something special that would last all year long."

"Can we can paste *anything* on our boxes?" Sam asked.

"Sure," Mom said.

"Anything at all?" I asked.

"Anything that you consider a special memory. That's why they will each be unique."

Possibilities raced through my mind.

Tori turned toward Mom. "Good idea. Maybe I'll make one, too."

"Yeah," I said. "You could use all those candy wrappers you have hidden in your drawer."

Tori's face turned red. "Piper Reed, you were snooping around in my drawer!"

"Look!" I pointed to the three jets in the sky. "The Blue Angels are practicing."

The jets flipped upside down for a moment before turning upright. Most Tuesday and Wednesday mornings, the Blue Angels practiced their flight formations. We could watch them from our backyard and the school playground. But my teacher didn't like us to watch them from our classroom window.

Last week when Ms. Gordon caught me watching, she said, "Piper, you need to be concentrating on your work right now."

Didn't she know I *was* concentrating on my work? After all, I planned to be a Blue Angel one day.

Tori still gave me the evil eye. I should have known the Blue Angels wouldn't make her lose focus. She was like a spider, spinning a web. Nothing could distract her. "Mom," she said, "it's not fair that Piper goes through my stuff."

Mom glanced at me in the rearview mirror.

"Your sister is right, Piper. Everyone should be able to have some privacy."

"Yes," Tori added. "That means you need to stay out of my room!"

I shrugged. "I got mixed up. I thought I was in *my* room." But really I didn't. It was easy to tell it wasn't my room. Tori was a slob. She threw clothes and junk on the floor until Chief made her pick up her mess. It had gotten worse since he'd left. Messes didn't bother Mom like they did Chief. Chief was known to dump stuff out of our drawers if we crammed too much in them. And by the end of the day, he expected everything to be folded and returned ship-shape.

On the rest of the way to school I thought about how I might decorate my memory box.

The Blue Angels' engines roared above. I'd start there—with the Blue Angels. My memory box was going to be truly spectacular.

At school my reading teacher, Ms. Mitchell, showed me a box of stickers. And they weren't those baby kind of stickers that Sam had plastered all over her notebooks. These stickers had the words u.s. NAVY and pictures of the Blue Angels.

Ms. Mitchell smiled and patted the pile of books on her desk. "For every book you finish you can select a packet."

I should have known there was a catch.

That afternoon, I practiced with Bruna again.

"Aahhh!" Sam was inside the house, but I could hear her scream all the way in the backyard. I dropped Bruna's biscuit and rushed to the kitchen.

Bruna wolfed down the biscuit and followed me. A second later, Mom and Tori joined us.

"What's wrong?" I asked Sam.

Sam stood on a chair, pointing at Peaches's bowl. "Peaches is dead!"

Sure enough, Peaches was floating sideways on the water's surface among a thick layer of fish-food flakes.

"What happened?" Tori asked.

"I don't know," cried Sam. "At first I thought

she was doing a new trick. I didn't even teach her to float. She did that on her own. So I gave her another treat."

"More flakes?" Mom's voice rose two octaves. "Oh, Sam honey, fish don't need that much food."

Now that I thought about it, I'd noticed Sam shaking fish flakes into Peaches's bowl twice that day already.

"You fed her to death," I said.

Sam sobbed again. "I killed Peaches!"

"Great, Piper!" Tori snapped. "You sure know how to make bad things worse!"

Mom picked up Sam like she was a baby. Her shoes dangled past Mom's knees. "It's okay, sweetie. We'll get you another fish."

Sam sniffed. "It won't be Peaches." Then she quickly asked, "Can we go to the pet store today?"

"After dinner," Mom promised.

So much for the memory of Peaches, I thought.

Sam slipped out of Mom's embrace, until she was standing on the floor. "But first Peaches needs a funeral."

"Flush!" I hollered.

"Pi-per." Mom gave me her better-not-say-another-word look. She settled on the edge of the tub and wrapped Peaches in toilet paper until Peaches was a mummy the size of a lumpy golf ball.

When she handed Peaches over to Sam, Sam asked, "Can I be alone with Peaches?"

"Sure." Mom guided Tori and me out of the bathroom and eased the door shut.

We waited in the hall.

I tapped my foot. "What's she doing in there?"

A minute later we heard the toilet flush. I was ticked. Sam didn't even wait for us to have the funeral, and I'd never been to a funeral before. I was kind of looking forward to it.

The door slowly opened, and Sam walked out.

"It's over," Sam said, staring down at the floor.

That evening we drove off-base and went to Sanchez's Land and Water Pals. Inside, puppies yelped and a parrot squawked, when it wasn't chanting "Pretty girl! Pretty girl!" I wanted to rush over to the snake terrarium, but Mom motioned me to the aquariums at the back of the store.

"Let's offer Sam support," she said.

"Can we get a snake?" I asked.

Mom peered down at me and frowned. I've learned there are two different types of people in the world—those who like snakes and those who quiver when you mention them. Mom was in the second group.

While Sam stared into the aquarium, Mr. Sanchez, the pet store owner, held the fishnet, ready for action.

"That one," she said, pressing her finger against the glass.

Mr. Sanchez dipped his fishnet into the tank and caught a goldfish.

Sam shook her head. "Nope. That one." She moved her finger to the other end of the tank.

Mr. Sanchez tried again.

"Nope," Sam said. "I want the one that looks like Peaches."

I sighed. "Sam, there are a hundred fish swimming in that tank and they're *all* the spitting image of Peaches."

"We're going to get the right one," Mr. Sanchez said. "Sanchez's Land and Water Pals guarantees to please." His round glasses were low on his nose, his focus fixed on the tank, as he moved the fishnet through the water. I'll bet Mr. Sanchez could easily win a no-blinking contest.

Finally he caught the fish that caused Sam to say, "Exactly!"

On the way home, Sam studied the fish swimming in the plastic bag. "I'm going to teach Peaches the Second lots of tricks," she said.

"You might want to lay off the treats this time," I told her. "Otherwise the only trick Peaches the Second will be doing is the floating one."

When I finished my memory box the next day, I set it on the desk and admired it. Every speck of the tissue box was covered. I included pictures of the Blue Angels that I'd cut from the brochure Chief and I picked up the day we went to the aviation museum. I added my drawing of our tree house in San Diego, a miniature sketch of my sand-castle design, and a picture of Chief in his uniform.

I centered the box on my desk and stared at it.

"Get off the bus," I whispered. My box was truly spectacular.

The school bell rang and I carried my memory box to the car. Mom had left earlier to pick up Tori at the middle school. They were waiting in the car for us. Tori finished her memory box the night before at home. She had to be first for everything, even when it wasn't her school assignment.

Her box was boring, of course. She'd pasted on lots of book titles she'd read and a picture of Margie Marcel, with long, curly black hair.

Soon Sam headed toward the car, taking long strides, pointing her toes as she lifted each leg. You would have thought she was leading a parade. She held out her box like a prize. When she got inside, a really bad odor overwhelmed the car.

"What stinks?" I asked.

Tori wrinkled her nose. "Yeah," she said. "What's that awful smell?"

Mom grimaced. "Show them your box, Sam."

Sam smiled real big and held up her box. "Ta-da!"

There, right in the middle of the seashells and flower petals, with its milky eyeball staring my way, was Peaches the First.

5

MARCH

It was spring break and we had the entire week off from school. Mom said it was time for another adventure. Somehow going on adventures made the months away from Chief go by a bit more quickly.

"We're going to New Orleans to visit Swoosie," she said.

Swoosie was Mom's favorite art teacher in college. We visited her years ago, but I couldn't remember her because I was too young.

"I hope we get to eat beignets at Café Du Monde," Tori said. Of course *Tori* remembered visiting New Orleans. She never forgot anything that had to do with food.

After school on Friday we packed our suitcases.

"Can we bring Bruna?" I asked. That way I could train her every day.

"Yeah," said Sam. "I want to bring Peaches the Second."

Mom shook her head. "I'm afraid not. Swoosie lives in a French Quarter apartment. There's no room for pets."

"But who will feed them?" I asked.

"Yolanda said she would look after them."

Early the next morning we got in the car and headed toward New Orleans. By noon, we had arrived at the French Quarter. Mom rolled down the windows so we could hear the bouncing beats of jazz playing on every street. The quarter smelled good and bad at the same time—spicy aromas like Mom's gumbo mixed with the stink of three-day-old trash.

We left the car inside a parking garage on Royal Street. Then we rolled our suitcases a few blocks, passing restaurants and antique shops, until we reached Swoosie's apartment. We rang the doorbell, but when Mom noticed the opened curtains, she stepped in front of the window and waved.

A tall woman waved back. "Just a second, honey!"

Swoosie opened the door. She wore a floral caftan and her red hair was twisted on top of her head. It was not like any red hair I'd ever seen—it was as bright as the stripes on the American flag.

Swoosie hugged Mom and said, "Honey, you look amazing. And your darling children. Come on in and have some iced tea."

We entered her apartment and she hugged each of us. Then we all settled on the couch while Swoosie sat in a black velvet chair.

"Three girls, Edie! My goodness, they're the spitting image of you."

"Except me," Sam said. "I'm the spitting image of Daddy."

"Come here. Let me see." Swoosie motioned to her until they were eyeball to eyeball. "Sure enough, you are."

Paintings covered every inch of Swoosie's walls. Art books were stacked in piles around the room on the floor next to more paintings. I guess Swoosie ran out of wall space. Some canvases showed the French Quarter's colorful buildings and iron railings. Others were abstract. That meant it looked like some little kid splashed paint on a canvas, but it was really about more. At least that's what Mom said. Most of them had Swoosie's loopy signature in the right-hand corner.

Across the room hung a painting of a young woman with flaming red hair and big earrings.

"Does that lady look familiar, Piper?" Swoosie asked.

I walked over for a closer look. "That's you, isn't it? You were a lot younger, though."

Mom gasped. "Piper!"

I forgot Mom and Chief had told us that old people don't want to be reminded that they're old.

Swoosie chuckled. "She's so right, Edie."

"It looks kind of like the way Mom paints," I said, noticing the broad bright strokes.

"You've got a good eye, Piper." Swoosie leaned forward and pointed at the painting. "Check out the artist's signature."

My eyes focused on the right-hand corner of the painting. It said Coco Kappel.

"Who's Coco?" I asked.

Swoosie raised her eyebrows. "You don't know who Coco Kappel is?"

I felt a blush crawl up my face.

I knew a lot of the

great artists—van Gogh, Matisse, O'Keeffe. Mom had told us about them since the day we were born. And we went to museums as much as some kids go to the movies. But I didn't know Coco Kappel. "Is she someone famous?"

Mom laughed, then hid her face with her hands.

Swoosie stretched out her arm toward Mom. "Ladies, may I present Coco Kappel."

Tori did a double take. "Mom?"

Mom shook her head. "Don't ask."

But I wanted to know all about Coco.

"Is Coco your real name?" Sam asked.

Mom chuckled. "I'll explain later."

Swoosie winked at Mom before heading toward the kitchen.

We ate jambalaya at a black iron table in Swoosie's courtyard. Then we went for a walk in the French Quarter. The damp air sent a chill through my skin all the way to my bones.

When we got to the end of the street, Swoosie told Mom, "Honey, this is as far as I go. You and the girls have fun. I'll be waiting for you when it's dinnertime."

We walked by Jackson Square, a pretty park with a statue of Andrew Jackson in the middle of it. Horse-pulled carriages were parked on the road that ran beside the square. Artists perched along the fence next to their easels. Some painted tourists' portraits, while others tried to sell their paintings to people who passed by. Mom was better than all of them. I couldn't wait to hear how she used to be Coco Kappel. We stopped walking when we reached Café Du Monde.

"Let's sit inside," Mom said.

"Oh," I whined. "Can't we sit outside like you did when you went to school here?"

"Please, Mommy," Sam begged. "Can't we sit outside?"

"Okay." Mom led us to a table under the covered patio.

Soon a waiter, wearing a white hat and apron, took our order. A few minutes later, he brought a tray with a plate of beignets—square doughnuts, covered in powdered sugar. He also brought us mugs of hot chocolate and Mom's café au lait.

"Can I try café au lait?" Sam asked.

"When you're older," Mom said.

"Why do I have to wait until I'm older?" Sam asked. "Is it bad for you?"

Mom shrugged her shoulders. "Not that bad, I guess. Here, have a sip." She held the mug for Sam. "Be careful, it's hot."

Sam straightened her shoulders, took a sip, then squinted. "Yuk!"

I reached across the table. "My turn."

Mom handed her mug to me. I swallowed. It was bitter and hot. "Sam's right," I said.

"Tori?" Mom offered her mug.

Tori held the mug with her pinky finger  pointing out. Her nose circled above the rim, as she took in a long sniff. Finally she closed her eyes and took a giant gulp of the café au lait. Her lip curled, but after she swallowed, she announced, "Scrumptious!"

Tori always liked to think she was grown up. We watched people pass by, but I kept stealing glances at Mom. To me, she looked just like a mom. Nothing unusual, nothing Coco Kappel about her at all.

I guess Mom noticed because she asked, "Piper, why are you staring at me?"

"I'm trying to figure it out."

"Figure what out?"

"Are you really Coco Kappel or not?"

She smiled. "I'm just plain ole Edie Reed or back then it was plain ole Edie Morris from Piney Woods, Louisiana. But I guess I wanted to be someone different, someone more exotic."

I knew exactly what Mom meant. Sometimes I wanted to be someone exotic, too. Maybe that's one of the reasons I want to be a Blue Angel.

"Some-times," Sam began slowly, "sometimes I want to be a fish."

Then we all cracked up, except for Sam who

folded her arms across her chest and frowned. I guess she was serious.

A half hour later, Sam was happy again because we went to the Audubon Aquarium of the Americas. We saw a zillion types of jellyfish. We watched the clowning otters and stingrays, which looked as if they were smiling. In another tank penguins swam near the glass and flapped their wings at us. We also saw a baby shark clinging to its mother's side. But the coolest thing of all was a terrarium with a king snake that had just shed its old skin.

When we saw a gold koi fish, Sam asked, "Do you think Peaches the Second could get that big?"

"No," I said. "She'd have to live a lot longer to get that big. Goldfish don't have a long life expectancy in the Reed household."

I thought Sam would get mad, but she just said, "Oh."

I had sounded mean and I felt bad. So I quickly added, "Of course, you never know. Peaches the Second could live to be as old as Swoosie or even a hundred."

We ate dinner at a restaurant called Irene's, which was just a short walk from Swoosie's street. And after dinner we returned to her apartment. We listened to Swoosie tell us stories about her life and the crazy people she knew. She'd visited every continent in the world and she'd met kings and danced with ambassadors.

When she came to the end of a story about her trip to Africa, Swoosie said, "I'm sorry, girls. I'm talked out and I'm sure you're worn out from listening."

Sam pointed to an item on a bookshelf. "Is that a magic wand?"

"Why, yes, it is." Swoosie went over to it

and handed the wand to Sam. "Push the button."

Sam did and a blinking light came on. "Oh my goodness! Oh my goodness!"

Swoosie laughed. "Sam, consider it yours. Every girl needs a little magic in her life."

Why did she give it to Sam? The Gypsy Club pet show would be here before I knew it, and I needed a little magic to help Bruna learn a trick.

That night Mom slept on the couch while Tori, Sam, and I slept in the guest bedroom. We had to share the bed. It was kind of fun, like having a slumber party even though it was with my sisters instead of friends.

Tori told us a story about a princess waiting for her prince. Suddenly we heard horse hooves clicking against the street outside our window. It was probably one of the horse-drawn carriages we'd seen earlier parked at Jackson

Square, but Tori lowered her voice and said, "Listen. There he is now."

"Who?" whispered Sam.

"The prince," Tori said.

I thought about ruining Tori's mushy story, but I changed my mind and kept quiet. That night I dreamed we were princesses living in a castle in the French Quarter. Our mother was Queen Coco. Tori was herself, but Sam looked exactly like Peaches the Second with a crown on her head. When a silly prince rode up on his horse, Tori acted so goofy. She probably wanted the prince to kiss her. And when he did, I take off on his horse and ride away.

We stayed at Swoosie's a couple more days. We visited Audubon Zoo, rode the ferry to the West Bank, and toured a factory where they build Mardi Gras floats. Then we hugged Swoosie good-bye and drove back to the base.

When we arrived home, I rushed out of the car and headed toward the front door. I couldn't wait to see Bruna.

"Don't forget your suitcase!" Mom hollered.

An hour later, Yolanda and Brady came over. Mom gave them a box of pralines.

"Did you have a good time?" Yolanda asked.

"We did," Mom answered. "Thank you for taking care of our pets. I hope Bruna wasn't any trouble."

"And Peaches the Second," Sam added. "I hope she wasn't any trouble either."

"Not at all," Yolanda said. "In fact, Brady taught Bruna a trick."

"What?!" I hadn't meant to yell, but I felt a sting as if a million bumblebees had attacked my insides.

Yolanda touched the top of Brady's head. "Brady, show them the trick you taught Bruna."

"Yes," Tori said. "Let's see your trick." She was facing Brady, but she peered at me out of the corner of her eyes.

Brady slipped his hand into his mother's pocket and pulled out a treat. Bruna came over immediately and sat, waiting across from Brady. Brady had the treat in one of his tiny fists. He placed his other hand on his hip and stayed quiet a long moment.

Bruna sat perfectly still, waiting.

Okay, I thought, where is this big trick?

Shaking his finger at Bruna, Brady ordered, "Woll over!"

Bruna fell to the ground and flipped over on her back.

Everyone clapped except me.

Then Brady gave Bruna the treat and said, "Good gwil!"

6

APRIL

Dear Dad,

    As your eldest daughter, I believe it's my duty to inform you that your wife, our beloved mother, fell down the stairs and broke her leg. I discovered her first. I promptly called Yolanda who took Mom to the hospital.

    I'm sure by now you're wondering how this could happen. I can explain it in two words. Piper Reed! As usual Piper was

snooping in *MY ROOM* and found my
journal. She took it out of *MY ROOM*
and left it on the stairs. Unfortunately,
Mom didn't see the journal. When she
stepped on it, she slid and fell to the
bottom of the stairs.

Please don't worry, Dad. I have
everything under control.

Your responsible eldest daughter,
Tori

Dear Daddy,
Mommy broke her leg.

Love,
Sam

P.S. It's Piper's fault.

Dear Chief,
I just read the e-mails Tori and Sam
sent to you. I need to set you straight.

Here's the **true** story.

I was looking for a pen in Tori's room and I accidentally stumbled on her journal. I didn't know it was a journal. I swear I didn't. But . . . it was open and a person can't help herself if someone leaves their journal open. I only read a tiny part. (Did you know that Tori had a crush on a boy named Ronnie Cartwright?)

While I was in her room, Sam walked by and said, "Um, I'm telling!"

"You're telling what?" I asked.

"You're reading Tori's journal," she said.

"No, I'm not," I explained. "I'm looking for a pen."

Then I grabbed a pen and left the room.

The next thing I knew, Mom was lying on the floor. Sam started crying and Tori said, "I don't know what to do. I don't know what to do." Sam and Tori were freaking out, until I said, "Quick, somebody call Yolanda." So that's exactly what Tori did.

This is what I think happened.

After I left Tori's room, Sam couldn't help herself. (Prodigies are that way. Curious.) She went back into Tori's room and took her journal. She was probably reading it on the stairs when she got nosy about something else and forgot to put it back. Don't worry, Dad. I'll take care of Mom. I'm not Tori. I don't freak out and I won't leave things on the floor like nosy Sam.

Love,
Piper (future Blue Angel
of the U.S. Navy)

P.S. I'm teaching Bruna some tricks so she'll win the Gypsy Club's pet show. We're having it in July so you can be there.

Chief sent us a short e-mail, the shortest one he'd ever sent.

> *Dear Girls,*
>   *I'll have to get to the bottom of this*
> *when I return home.*

Sam's eyes grew big when she read what Chief wrote. "What does 'get to the bottom of this' mean?" she asked.

I told her, "It means someone is in big trouble."

Grandma Morris and Uncle Leo arrived Saturday from Louisiana to help take care of Mom. Uncle Leo, Mom's brother, was a hummingbird expert. He'd recently visited Mexico, where he took pictures of the Striped-tailed Hummingbird. Uncle Leo traveled the world, chasing humming-birds and teaching others about them.

Mom called the gate guard at the base entrance and gave Grandma and Uncle Leo's names so they'd be allowed on the base.

"When the gate guards see Uncle Leo they might not let him on the base," Sam said.

Sam never forgot the first time she saw Uncle Leo with his homemade hummingbird attractor hat. It was really a motorcycle helmet with purple and red silk flowers glued on it so he could attract hummingbirds. The best part was the attached hose with a squeeze button that sprayed a sweet floral scent on the blooms. Uncle Leo probably looked real scary to most little kids with his helmet and thick red beard and mustache. Once, a hummingbird got caught in his beard.

It rained the Saturday Grandma Morris and Uncle Leo arrived. Grandma shook off the rain, gave us each a hug, then said, "Where's my baby?" She wasn't talking about Sam. She was talking about Mom.

Grandma was shorter than Tori. But whenever anyone joked about her height, she snapped, "Dynamite comes in small packages."

When they arrived, Mom was sitting on the couch with her leg propped on the coffee table.

"That leg needs a pillow under it." Grandma grabbed a couple of throw pillows from the couch and slid them under Mom's pink cast.

"Thanks, Mother," Mom said.

Grandma swung around and faced us. "Leo, bring in the luggage. Girls, make room for my stuff in one of the closets. Tori, shut out the public." That was her way of saying "Pull down the blinds."

Chief always joked that Grandma Morris had missed her calling. "We could have used her in the Navy," he'd said. Then he added, "On second thought, let's give that privilege to the U.S. Army."

After she hung up her clothes, Grandma asked, "What time is it?"

"Nineteen thirty," I said.

Her hands flew to her hips. "In civilian talk, please."

"Seven thirty," Sam said.

"Goodness' sakes alive! We're missing *Wheel of Fortune*." Grandma rushed into the living room and grabbed the remote control from the coffee table, barely missing Mom's toes sticking out from her cast.

If this had been Grandma Reed, she would have headed straight toward the kitchen and turned on the oven. Grandma Reed's idea of showing love was to stuff us like a Thanksgiving turkey. But Grandma Morris thought there was no reason to heat up the house with a hot stove when the microwave could heat a plateful of nachos in thirty seconds flat.

I settled on the couch next to Mom. Grandma was sitting in Chief's recliner with her feet straight out.

The TV show host said, "Name something you do in a movie theater."

The first two things the contestants named were wrong.

Grandma shook her head. "Gracious, don't those folks know anything you do at the movie theater?"

"Eat popcorn!" I yelled.

"That's using your noodle, Piper," Grandma said.

"Watch the movie!" Sam hollered.

Grandma winked at her. "You always were a smart gal, Sam."

"Make out in the back row," Tori said.

"Why, of course," Grandma said, then turned and frowned at Tori. "Get your head out of the gutter, Tori."

The next morning, Grandma stayed home and watched *Good Morning, America* while Uncle Leo drove the four of us to school. After he dropped off Tori at her middle school, he drove to our school and parked. Then he carried Mom's supplies into the building while she hobbled behind us on her crutches. Later, Uncle Leo picked us up in the afternoon.

"Did you bring your hummingbird attractor hat?" I asked him.

"Of course," he said, as if he'd never left home without it.

"Could you be my show-and-tell this week, Uncle Leo?"

"I don't know. What is show-and-tell?"

Mom always said Uncle Leo lived in his own world. I guess they didn't have show-and-tell on that planet. I explained it all to him. "It's where you stand in front of the entire class and show or talk about something. So I would say, 'This is my uncle Leo and he's an expert on hummingbirds. He's just returned from Mexico, where he studied the Striped-tailed Hummingbird.' Then you talk about it."

Uncle Leo paused, pushing at the bridge of his glasses. "Certainly," he said. "It's always my pleasure to talk about hummingbirds."

I could hardly wait until Friday. Uncle Leo would be the best show-and-tell of the year. Thursday night, Tori said I was absolutely crazy to invite Uncle Leo to school wearing that "ridiculous" hat.

I told her, "You're just jealous because you don't have show-and-tell in the seventh grade."

"Thank heavens for small blessings," she said.

Finally the end of the week arrived. As usual, Uncle Leo drove Tori to her middle school first. Then he took the rest of us to school.

"I want Uncle Leo to be *my* show-and-tell," Sam said. I guess she'd gotten over being afraid of him.

"Too bad," I said. "I asked first."

Uncle Leo's posture straightened. "I'd be

happy to be your show-and-tell next week, Sam."

"Superb!" Sam dashed off to class while Uncle Leo and I headed toward mine.

Everyone gawked at Uncle Leo and me as we walked down the hall and into my classroom. Maybe they were staring at Uncle Leo's black socks and Bermuda shorts. Or maybe they were just impressed with his amazing hum-mingbird hat.

"The better to attract hummingbirds," he'd explained to me earlier.

I pulled up a desk and chair for Uncle Leo. The fit was tight, but he finally squeezed in.

When Ms. Gordon arrived, she jumped back a bit and said, "Oh, my! I didn't know we had a guest this morning."

"This is my uncle Leo," I said. "He's my show-and-tell."

"Okay," Ms. Gordon said slowly as her eyelid began to quiver. It always seemed to happen when she talked to me.

"Well," Ms. Gordon said. "We usually have show-and-tell at the end of the day. But since we have a guest today, I think we'll do it first thing. Piper, why don't you start us off?"

"No, thank you."

"Pardon?"

"I mean, no, ma'am, thank you. I'd like to go last." That way show-and-tell would end with a big finish. Uncle Leo was like the last M&M in a bag. It's always the best.

Ms. Gordon's mouth dropped as if she was going to say something, but nothing came out. Then she said, "Okay. Who wants to go first?"

Nicole raised her hand and then she went to the front of the class. She stood up straight and smiled real big, revealing her purple rubber bands on her braces.

"Nicole," Ms. Gordon said. "What is your show-and-tell?"

Nicole kept smiling and pointing to her teeth. Then she said, "I got purple."

Ms. Gordon nodded. "Yes, I see that, Nicole. Now what is your show-and-tell?"

"That's it." Nicole returned to her seat.

Michael groaned and buried his head in his arms.

Ms. Gordon sighed. "Okay. Anyone else?"

Silence.

"Your turn, Piper." Gosh. It seemed like Ms. Gordon could hardly wait for me to get up there.

Uncle Leo struggled to get out of the desk, knocking it over when he finally managed to stand.

Butterflies flew inside my belly as I made my way to the front of the room with him. "This is my uncle Leo and he's an expert on hummingbirds. Today, he's going to tell you about the Striped-tailed Hummingbird from Mexico."

Uncle Leo opened his briefcase and pulled out a stack of papers. He must have forgotten that he was doing show-and-tell to a bunch of fourth-graders because he started to read a speech. I guess it was the same speech he read at all those lectures he gave at museums and colleges. I didn't think you could make a subject as cool as hummingbirds boring, but Uncle Leo managed to do it just fine. The only interesting part was when he finally demonstrated his hummingbird attractor hat. He squeezed the button and . . .

It's too bad that Ms. Gordon chose that exact moment to step a bit too close. I tried to warn her, but I think she wanted to tell Uncle Leo that his time was up. After all, it was the longest show-and-tell presentation we'd ever had. When Uncle Leo pushed the button, the liquid traveled through the hose and flew out, spraying Ms. Gordon in the face. Her nose twitched like a rabbit's. She began to sneeze and sneeze. She sneezed as she dug in her purse. She sneezed while Nicole snatched a tissue out of her backpack and offered it to her. Ms. Gordon sneezed so much, she had to leave the classroom.

At first I thought she'd gone to the bathroom,

but a few minutes later the assistant principal, Mr. Howard, arrived and told us, "I'm afraid Ms. Gordon had to go home. She had an allergic reaction."

Nicole raised her hand.

Mr. Howard nodded to her. "Yes?"

"I have a lot of allergies. What is Ms. Gordon allergic to?"

"I think she said, 'Pepper.' That's what it sounded like she was saying anyway. 'Pepper, pepper,' she said. And her poor eyelid kept quivering. I'm sure she'll be just fine, but I told her to go home and get some rest. I've called a substitute for the class, but it will be this afternoon before she arrives. Meanwhile, I've arranged for the class to watch a movie on DVD."

When Mr. Howard said that, the kids clapped. My insides bubbled. Uncle Leo had ended up being entertaining after all.

Uncle Leo visited Sam's kindergarten class

the next week, but he had to leave early because a couple of the kids started crying when he put on his hummingbird attractor hat. One kid even peed his pants.

By the weekend, Grandma Morris and Uncle Leo were gone. Not because Mom's leg had healed. She still had another month to wear her cast. They left because the greatest thing in the world happened. Chief came home!

Chief was not supposed to come home until May. We had planned all kinds of things for his return. We'd even made a list.

1. Surprise Chief by decorating the house with balloons and a banner that read WEL-COME HOME, DAD!
2. Drive to the base in Mayport, where Chief's ship would come in, and meet Chief on the dock.

3. Sam planned to kiss Chief first.
4. Give Chief a preview of one of Bruna's tricks that she'd perform at the Gypsy Club pet show.

Instead, this is what happened:
1. Chief surprised us! We opened the door and there he stood. The ship's captain let Chief come home two weeks early.
2. Chief said, "I want a hug and kiss from all my girls, but first I have to get one from my favorite girl." (I was busy wondering if he meant me or Tori or Sam  when Chief walked across the room and lifted Mom off the sofa and gave her the

longest kiss in history. It was longer than any of the ones I'd seen in those mushy movies.)

3. Tori said, "How romantic!"

4. I said, "Yuk!"

5. Sam said, "I did it! I didn't mean to, but I forgot and left Tori's journal on the stairs. Please don't get to the bottom of it!"

6. I didn't give Chief a preview of one of Bruna's tricks because Bruna still didn't know how to do one. (Unless Brady asked her.)

7

May

The only bad thing about Chief coming home was now there were five people waiting for the bathroom most mornings instead of four. The beginning of the last week of school I stood outside the bathroom, my legs crossed, waiting for Tori to finish.

Suddenly Tori let out a squeal. "Aaah!"

I opened the door, but she leaned against it from the other side and yelled, "Stay out!"

I pushed with all my might before she

slammed the door shut. It was too late. I'd already stole a glimpse of the big red bump on her nose. It was bigger than a mosquito bite, redder than a wart. Tori Reed had a pimple.

Mom reached the bathroom just as we heard the door lock click. She'd gotten her cast removed last week and was wearing her periwinkle sneakers. "Tori?"

Tori unlocked the door and cracked it open wide enough for one eyeball to peer out.

"Mom only," Tori ordered.

Sam showed up about the time that Mom slipped inside the bathroom, and a few minutes later Tori came out with a bandage across the bridge of her nose.

"What happened?" Sam asked.

"None of your business," Tori snapped.

Sam looked hurt. Tori usually saved all her screaming for me.

"A pimple," I explained. "Tori got her first pimple."

All the way to school, I made up songs. It was easy when you put the words to a perfectly good tune. I sang, "A Pimple on the Nose," to the tune of "The Farmer and the Dell." And "How'd You Get that Big Red Pimple?" to the tune of "How Much Is That Doggy in the Window?"

I was having a great time until Mom said, "Okay, Piper, enough. Your day will come."

"Nope," I said. "I'm never going to have a pimple."

Mom stared at me through the rearview mirror. I knew she wasn't happy because she raised her left eyebrow when she said, "You'll hardly have any control over that."

"I hope you get a zillion pimples all over your body," Tori said.

Sam giggled. "Then we can call you Polka-Dotted Piper."

Usually I liked leaving class for Ms. Mitchell's. When everyone else was in the middle of doing boring work, I got to escape to Ms. Mitchell's cool room with purple walls and a yellow bean-bag chair. I got to do that every day just because I had dyslexia.

One day, though, we were right in the middle of watching a movie about the food chain. The movie came to the part where the snake was about to eat the frog when Ms. Mitchell showed up. The highlight of the year and I had to miss it! I'd never seen a snake swallow a frog before and I was really looking forward to it. I wondered what happened to a snake's belly with a frog inside it. Would there be a lump in the shape of a frog? Instead of slithering around, did his insides start jumping until the frog had been digested? I sure hoped Michael remembered all the cool details for me.

We reached Ms. Mitchell's room, and I settled in the beanbag chair.

"Piper, your reading has improved greatly this last month. I'm so proud of you." When Ms. Mitchell said that, it made me want to pick up a thick book and read it, cover to cover. But then she handed the summer reading list to me and I quickly changed my mind.

"You mean I have to read all these books this summer?" Her list covered two typed pages, longer than any of Chief's.

Ms. Mitchell smiled. "You need to select eight. Piper, you're very capable of reading that amount. You've accomplished a lot this school year."

Now I regretted trying so hard. And it all

had been for those silly stickers. I stared at the list. I think Ms. Mitchell gave me that long list just so I'd think eight books weren't that many. Eight books were a lot. I decided I'd find out how many pages each of the books had. Then I planned to pick the eight shortest.

After our session, I returned to my classroom. It was art day and Mom was already there. "Take your seat, Piper. We're just about to start sculpting."

Sure enough, a clump of clay was on top of my desk. My fingers felt itchy. This was the project I'd waited for all year. It was no secret. Everyone knew I was a champion Play-Doh sculptor. But this was the real deal.

"What do we sculpt?" Michael asked.

"Anything you want," Mom said. "Anything can be your inspiration—birds, your mom's face, a pet."

"I'm going to sculpt my dog," Hailey said.

Good idea, I thought. I could sculpt Bruna. Then I could place the sculpture next to the trophy she was going to win at the Gypsy Club pet show.

But try as I did, I couldn't concentrate on Bruna. There was only one thing that I could think about. Oh well, I thought. Inspiration could come from anyplace. Mom even said it.

I started squeezing, letting my fingers get the feel of the cool clay. Then I began my masterpiece.

A few minutes later, Matthew looked over at my project. "Get off the bus! Those nostrils look real!"

"Thank you," I said, not bothering to glance up. My fingers smoothed down the bridge.

"That sure is a big nose," Nicole said. "It kind of makes me feel like I need to sneeze.

Aaaa-aaaa-choo!" She dug in her desk for a package of tissues. "I hope I'm not getting the flu."

Hailey walked over to my desk for a closer look. "Aren't you going to do the whole face?"

"Nope," I said, rolling a smaller piece of clay into a ball. When I got it just right, I plopped it on the right side of the nose.

"What's that?" Hailey asked. "A wart?"

"A pimple!" shouted Michael. "Piper made a big pimple on a nose." Then he cracked up.

Nicole's hand flew to her right nostril. "Oh, no. I don't have an ugly pimple, do I?"

Mom came over and stared at my project. She sighed.

I shrugged. "You said inspiration could come from anywhere."

"Yes, but . . ."

Hailey held up her clay sculpture. "Look at my dog, Mrs. Reed."

Mom walked to Hailey's desk and inspected her creation. "That's marvelous."

I studied Hailey's sculpture, the small pointy ears, the wispy whiskers, the short hair, and the long tail. "That looks like a cat," I said.

Hailey frowned. "It's a dog. It looks just like my dog, Buttercup."

"Does Buttercup say meow?" I asked.

"You're just jealous, Piper Reed, because my dog is going to win the pet show."

I shrugged. "You might have a shot since it's not a beauty contest."

"Piper," Mom said, "that's enough."

It's tough when your mom is the art teacher because she can't tell everyone that your project is marvelous, the best in the class, even if it is.

Later, on the ride home, I showed Tori my project.

Tori's eyebrows touched as she studied the perfect image of her nose. Then her eyes got big, real big, as if she'd just figured out what my sculpture was.

"Mom!" she yelled. "How could you let Piper do that in front of her whole class?"

Mom sighed. "No one knew it was your nose, Tori."

"You can have it," I told Tori. "A celebration of your first pimple."

She glared at me like I was the devil. "I don't want it!" She turned away, then suddenly swerved back in my direction. "Wait! Yes, I do. Give it to me."

Before I could hand her my sculpture, she

grabbed it, rolled down the window, and threw it out.

I turned and watched the car behind us drive over my masterpiece and smash the nostrils into a flat pancake. Some people have no appreciation for true art.

8

JUNE

The first day of summer vacation, I slipped out of bed early while the rest of my family slept. The books I'd chosen to read from the summer reading list were on my nightstand. There were eight, but there might as well have been a hundred. The only book that looked interesting was about a dog named Shiloh. But even it had to wait. I needed to prepare for my big win.

There was a month left until the Gypsy Club pet show. Unfortunately, Bruna knew half a trick. Well, one and a half if I counted the rollover trick Brady taught her. But I wanted to teach Bruna a trick all by myself.

I fed Bruna and gave her some water, then took her outside to do her business. The sun was starting to climb in the sky. In the distance, I heard "The Star-Spangled Banner" play. Morning colors happened every day at o-eight hundred. All around the base, the American flags had just been raised. While the national anthem played I stood perfectly still, my left arm to my side, my right hand at a salute, facing the flag across the street. Even civilians on the base remained quiet during this time. They didn't have to salute like personnel in uniform, but I always did. Besides, it was good practice for when I became a Blue Angel.

After the song finished, the whistle blew three short pipes.

"Carry on," I said to myself, refocusing on Bruna.

Then I heard a shout from next door.

"Hi, Piper!" Brady waved his entire arm. He sat in his miniature lawn chair on his front porch next to Yolanda.

"Hi, Brady. Hi, Yolanda."

"I'm almost twee!" Brady said, holding up three fingers.

"That's right, Brady," I said. "You're almost a big boy."

"Whatcha doing?" Brady asked.

"Teaching Bruna a trick."

"Can I watch?" he asked.

"Sure," I said, but I really didn't want him to.

I unsnapped Bruna's leash from her collar. Nine treats hid in my pocket. I was ready.

I threw the ball across the yard. "Fetch, Bruna!"

Bruna raced to the ball, and just as she always did, she picked it up and circled the yard.

"Here, Bruna!" I yelled. "Give it here!"

But Bruna ignored me and kept running.

"Here, Bruna," I ordered, this time sounding like bossy Tori. My face burned, knowing that Yolanda and Brady were watching me fail.

Suddenly Brady hollered, "Here, Boona!"

Bruna slowed her pace and stopped. Then she headed straight to Brady and dropped the ball at his feet.

Brady reached down and patted Bruna's head. "Good gwil," he said.

I sighed.

Later that day, the Gypsy Club met at my home.

"We need an MC for the pet show," Michael said.

"What's an MC?" I asked.

"The master of ceremonies. That's the person

who's in charge of introducing us and our pets."

"It should be someone older," said Hailey.

"How about Tori?" Nicole asked.

I thought about the times I'd caught Tori talking in front of the mirror, pretending that someone was interviewing her. "Yeah," I said, "she could do it." I went to tell her.

A few moments later, Tori came to my door with a notebook. And a few seconds later, you would have thought she'd made up the entire Gypsy Club pet show.

"Here's the order of how everyone will come onstage," she said, showing her list.

"We don't have a stage," I said.

Tori sighed and rolled her eyes. If there was a world record for the most times that a person rolled their eyes, Tori would be the champion.

"We can throw down a sheet. That can be the stage." She studied her notebook. "And we need a judge."

"Judge?" I'd forgotten about a judge.

"Oh, no," Nicole said. "We don't have a judge."

Tori folded her arms across her chest. "Well, it is a contest, isn't it?"

"Yes," I said. "There will be a winner." Only now I wasn't so sure that winner would be Bruna. I had tried and tried to teach her some tricks. But she wouldn't do any of them unless Brady was around.

"I could ask a friend," Tori offered.

"That wouldn't be fair," Hailey said. "Your friend would probably pick Piper."

Tori smirked. "Probably not," Tori said, "but it's your decision. Who do you suggest then?"

All of a sudden I thought of the perfect judge. "How about Mr. Sanchez? He owns a pet store."

Tori smiled. "Good thinking, Piper."

That was the first time my sister had ever said that to me.

When the Gypsy Club meeting ended, Tori went to call Mr. Sanchez while I practiced with Bruna. I was filled with hope every time Bruna chased after the ball and picked it up. Then my hopes quickly crashed when she raced around the yard, ignoring my voice.

"Here, Bruna." I had given up the arm signal. Brady never used it and Bruna always did the trick for him.

That's when it came to me. Right there in the middle of the yard, I realized what it would take to win the first annual Gypsy Club pet show. All I needed was an assistant. An assistant who was almost three. An assistant named Brady.

9

JULY

The base's July Fourth celebration was a few days before the Gypsy Club pet show.

We ate hamburgers and hot dogs and dug our hands into the ice-filled plastic garbage cans for soft drinks. Some of the men and women played baseball, including Chief.

He hit a home run, then ran off the field and grabbed Mom, who was standing near the bleachers. And even though he'd been back for more than a month, he swung her around and said, "It's great to be home!"

When he said that, it made me wonder. *Where was our real home?* Right now NAS Pensacola was home. Last year San Diego was home. Before that, it was Guam. I guess when you're in the Navy, anyplace you live is home, but never for long.

That afternoon, the Blue Angels performed a flight demonstration. My favorite part was the Delta Formation that took six jets. When I became a Blue Angel, I'd probably be assigned the Diamond Formation first since it only took four jets.

When the sun went down there was a fireworks show. During the finale the sky lit up with red, white, and blue. I cupped my hands around my mouth and yelled "Get off the bus!" louder than I'd ever yelled. But no one could hear me because of the popping sounds of the fireworks, the music playing, and the applause. After that we headed home. It was twenty-three hundred by the time we arrived. Chief had to carry Sam to our room because she'd fallen asleep in the car.

In bed I thought about the day. I decided the Fourth of July was my favorite holiday next to Christmas and my birthday.

"One day I'm going to fly with the Blue Angels," I whispered to Sam. Of course she didn't hear me since she was already asleep.

"But first," I added, "I'm going to win the

Gypsy Club pet show." Now I was confident that Bruna and I would win. Because now I had a secret weapon.

Finally, Saturday arrived. Chief set up chairs in the backyard and spread out a sheet that would be our stage. Before breakfast, I heard Tori practicing her lines through the bedroom vent. "Welcome to the first Gypsy Club pet show. I'm Tori Reed, your master of ceremonies for the event." Blah, blah, blah.

A moment later, Tori dropped her voice. "Good afternoon. Welcome to the annual Gypsy Club . . ."

I hated to admit it, but she did sound just like one of those ladies on the news. Maybe Tori would grow up and be a television news reporter. Then she could interview me and the other Blue Angels.

People started to arrive for the show a half hour early. Ms. Austin parked and got out of her car with Michael and Nicole. Michael carried his guinea pig in one hand and a paper sack in the other.

"What's in there?" I asked.

"You'll see."

"Is it a secret?"

"Let's just say I don't want to let all my tricks out of the bag."

"Ha-ha," I said. I peered over at Brady's yard, but there was no sign of him. I hoped he'd show up soon with Yolanda and Abe. Brady had seemed so excited when I asked him to be my assistant at the show.

"Okay," he'd said. "I be you sis-tent." We'd even practiced four times.

Nicole had her cat on a leash. It looked like it weighed fifty pounds.

"Wow," I said. "Your cat must like to eat."

"Shelby's just fluffy," she said. "She's really not that big."

Some of Tori's friends came with a boy who looked familiar. Then I realized the skinny boy with scraped knees was Ronnie Cartwright, the boy Tori wrote about in her journal. I recognized him because she'd drawn a heart around his picture in her yearbook. Yuk!

Finally Yolanda, Abe, and Brady walked over. My stomach flip-flopped. I hoped my plan would work.

Hailey was late. If she didn't hurry we'd have to start without her. And that meant she'd be disqualified. But Mr. Sanchez hadn't arrived either. How could I win the Gypsy Club pet show if the judge didn't show up?

Tori appeared, though when she saw Ronnie Cartwright sitting in the front row, her face turned the color of a tomato. "Uh, hi," she said.

Ronnie tilted his head to the side, causing his long bangs to cover his eyes. "Hey."

Tori's friend Kate spoke so fast, her words ran together. "Ronnie said he wanted to see the pet show, and we didn't think you'd mind." Then she smacked her bubblegum.

Tori froze. She was probably wishing she'd worn her blue eye shadow and lip gloss, but of course she couldn't. Mom and Chief would have grounded her.

"No makeup until you're fifteen," Mom had said when she found out sneaky Tori was putting it on at school.

Suddenly we heard a sputtering sound. A purple van with animals and fish painted on it made its way down the street. The van moved with a bounce and the muffler spit out *putt-putt-putt* until it parked in front of our house. The letters on the van read SANCHEZ'S LAND AND WATER PALS. A second later, Mr. Sanchez got out.

He wore sunglasses, but his eyeglasses were positioned atop his head.

Mom greeted him. "Mr. Sanchez, it's so kind of you to judge the show."

"Sanchez's Land and Water Pals goes beyond the call of duty." He tucked his notebook under his arm and followed Mom to the backyard.

"Where's Hailey?" Michael asked.

"I don't know," I said. "We might have to start the show without her."

"We're here!" Hailey was walking into our backyard with her dog on a leash. I didn't care what she said—her dog did look like a cat. A very ugly cat.

"Sorry that Buttercup and I are late," she said. "My mom had to drive my brother to baseball practice first. She parked the car down the street, but she'll be here in a minute."

Nicole's cat, Shelby, hissed and arched her back at Buttercup.

Buttercup cowered and hid behind Hailey's legs.

Nicole tugged at the leash. "No, no, Shelby."

"We can start now," I told Tori. "Everyone is here."

Tori took a big breath. Then she began, "Okay. Ladies and gentlemen, welcome"—she stared straight ahead at Ronnie— "um . . . welcome to the . . . the . . ."

"The Gypsy Club pet show," I whispered.

"The Gypsy Club pet show," Tori repeated. "I'm . . . I'm . . ."

"TORI REED!" I hollered. Everyone laughed.

"I'm Tori Reed, the master of ceremonies."

I wished Ronnie wasn't at our pet show. Why couldn't he go skateboarding somewhere far from our backyard? He made Tori so nervous, she couldn't even remember her own name.

"First up is Sam Reed."

Sam rolled her Radio Flyer wagon over to the stage. Inside the wagon, Peaches the Second sloshed with the water in the fishbowl. Sam placed the bowl on a small table. Then she picked up her magic wand and turned on the switch that lit it up.

"Ladies and gentlemen, watch carefully as Peaches the Second follows directions," Sam said. She tapped the right side of the bowl. Peaches the Second swam over to the wand. Sam lowered it to the bottom of the fishbowl. "Now swim here." Peaches the Second swam to the bottom.

"Over here," Sam commanded. Again and

again, Sam tapped the glass with her wand in different spots of the bowl. Again and again, Peaches the Second followed the blinking light.

She would've continued tapping that fishbowl if I hadn't hollered, "Good job! Thanks! Next!"

"Ta-da!" Sam said, her arms wide apart, reaching toward the sky. Then she bowed low.

Everyone clapped.

Sam curtsied.

The audience continued to clap, probably because they didn't know what else to do.

Then, as if someone pushed the replay button, Sam started to use her wand again.

"Time's up!" I yelled.

Sam ignored me, tapping the glass with her wand. *Ting, ting, ting.*

"That's enough, Sam!" I shouted.

Sam's hands flew to her waist. "There's no time limit."

"Yes, there is," I said. "And you better stop now or you'll be disqualified."

Sam twirled. "But I haven't done my encore yet."

Chief cupped his hand around his mouth. "Great job, Sam."

She curtsied again. "Thanks, Daddy."

"Now take a seat," said Mom.

Sam carefully placed the fishbowl in the wagon and rolled it offstage.

Tori took her place in the center. "Next up is Nicole and her cat, Shelby."

Nicole walked to the stage with Shelby and undid her leash. "Shelby will now demonstrate her yo-yo trick."

But before Nicole could slip the yo-yo string around her finger, Shelby arched her back and hissed at Buttercup. When Buttercup got a look at Nicole's mad fat cat, she took off running.

Shelby chased Buttercup out of the yard and

down the sidewalk. Hailey and Nicole took off
after their pets.

A few chuckles came from the audience, followed by silence.

"Well," Tori said. "Maybe we should move on
for now. Piper Reed and Bruna, please come up
to the stage."

What? I wasn't ready yet. I was supposed to be last. Michael and his guinea pig were next. That way, the show would have a spectacular ending. I was about to protest. Then I thought about it. How could a guinea pig top Bruna? Especially now that I had my secret weapon.

When I reached the stage I called out, "Would Brady please come to the stage?"

That's when I noticed that Brady had fallen asleep on Yolanda's lap. His head rested on her shoulder and a string of drool hung from his mouth.

"Brady," Yolanda said softly. "Wake up, Brady. It's your turn to help Piper."

Brady rubbed his eyes. "I go night-night."

Yolanda jiggled her knees and Abe said, "You can go night-night in a little while. Help Piper first."

Brady hid his face in Yolanda's shoulder and whined, "I want to go night-night!"

Yolanda looked helpless. Bruna went over to Brady and licked his toes.

Brady kicked his legs. "No, no, NO!"

Abe shrugged. "Sorry, Piper. What can we do? He's only two."

"He's almost twee," I blurted. "I mean three."

"We're sorry," Yolanda said, "but I'm sure you'll do just fine without him."

I froze and studied all the faces staring back at me that seemed to be waiting for Bruna to do something wonderful. I took a deep breath and guided Bruna to the stage. Then I tucked my hand in my pocket and dug out a dog biscuit.

Bruna sat waiting for a treat.

But I needed to show her who was boss. "Stay."

To my surprise, she stayed at perfect attention, her gaze fixed on my pocket.

I gave her the treat. "Good girl."

Then I shook my finger and said, "Roll over!"

Again, she shocked me by lying on her side and rolling on her back. The audience broke out in applause.

"Get off the bus!" I felt proud and I looked over at Chief. He was grinning. Bruna and I were stars!

"Good girl," I said, digging in my pocket for another treat.

Nothing could stop me now. I threw the ball. "Fetch, Bruna!"

Bruna ran after the ball, picked it up, and started running around the yard.

"Here, Bruna!" I yelled.

Finally Bruna raced toward me.

Here she comes. Here she comes. My heart pounded.

"Good girl," I said, a little too soon because just as she reached me she turned and made another lap around the yard.

The audience laughed.

"HERE!" I called out, bringing my arm straight down to my side.

Sam stood in the audience. "Time's up!"

"That's right, Piper," Tori said. "Time's up."

"But . . ."

"You did great, Piper!" Chief said, "but now it's Michael's turn."

I felt like I was going to throw up. I walked

off the stage and returned to my seat. Just as Michael stepped on the stage, Bruna stopped running, came over to me, and dropped the ball at my feet. I glanced around to see if anyone noticed, but all eyes were focused on Michael.

"You have bad timing, Bruna," I grumbled. Then I dug in my pocket and gave her a treat anyway.

Michael opened the sack and pulled out a CD player. He eased his guinea pig into a clear plastic ball with holes. Then he turned on the music and moved to the side, leaving his guinea pig in the center of the stage.

He scooped his left arm down and swept it in the direction of the guinea pig. "Presenting Tippy Toes and the Tango."

The music began and Tippy Toes moved the ball by moving his tiny legs. The ball rolled and rolled. When the music changed tempo, Tippy Toes stopped, turned around, and moved the

ball in the other
direction. Tippy
Toes, the guinea
pig, was moving
to the music.

"Dance! Dance!"
yelled Brady, who was
now wide awake, clapping.

Everyone else applauded, too. Leave it to
Michael to have the only guinea pig in
Pensacola, Florida, that could do the tango.

When the music ended, Tippy Toes stopped
moving. Michael picked up the ball and bowed.
Even from where I sat, I could see Tippy Toes
twitch his nose.

Suddenly Hailey and Nicole returned with
their pets. All four were soaked from head to
toe. The girls' wet shoes made squeaky noises as
they moved closer to the audience.

Hailey put her hands on her hips and stared

at me. "Did you ask all your neighbors to water their lawns on Saturdays at the same time?" She removed her shoes and poured out little puddles.

Nicole just stood there, sneezing. "I don't think Shelby is going to feel like performing her tricks today."

I looked down at Shelby. Nicole was right. Her cat wasn't fat after all. She looked like a skinny wet rat.

Hailey now had Buttercup on a leash. This time, when Shelby arched her back and hissed at Buttercup, Buttercup ran circles around Hailey until the leash wound up around her tightly and she fell straight over like a log that's just been cut.

Flat on her back, Hailey stared at the sky. "Well, Piper Reed," she said, "you certainly know how to deal with the competition. There's no way Buttercup could go on now."

I shrugged. "Suit yourself."

A moment later, Mr. Sanchez went to the stage with his notebook. "This was a difficult decision."

When he said that, a few adults chuckled.

He continued. "But the winner of the first annual Gypsy Club pet show goes to Tippy Toes. In all my years I've never witnessed a more talented guinea pig. And I've seen a lot of guinea pigs in my life."

Today we'd discovered a cat that looked like a rat, a dog that looked like a cat, and a guinea pig that danced the tango. This was the best pet show ever!

Everyone applauded while Michael went up to the stage and received the trophy. Even though Michael and Tippy Toes won, I didn't care. Because, better than that, Bruna had done her tricks for me. Just for me. Now all I had to do was work on her timing.

10

AUGUST

Eight. That's how many days remained until school started. That's also how many books were left to read from my reading list. All summer I ignored the stack of books, hoping they would disappear. First there was the Gypsy Club pet show. Then I took four weeks of swimming lessons. Every day I learned something new. Now I could dog-paddle, swim underwater, and do the breaststroke. I hadn't had time to read any of those books.

"Why don't you start with *Shiloh*?" Mom had suggested. "That's the one you're most interested in anyway."

"I want to save the best for last." Maybe then, I'd thought, that would make me hurry and read the others. Now I didn't want to read any of them. And why hadn't Ms. Mitchell put more dog books on the list anyway? Or why not some about the Blue Angels? Then at least I would have had a few good choices.

"You know you'll have to read every day to try to finish before school starts," Mom said.

"I'll never finish, even if I read all day."

"At least you can say you tried."

Tori scowled. "It's only eight books!" When she said that, it made me feel real dumb.

Later, Chief announced we'd be going to the beach for an end-of-the-summer vacation.

"Do we get to stay in the spaceship?" I asked.

He smiled and glanced at Mom. "How'd you ever guess, Piper?"

I was excited. So was Sam, and even Tori, too. Chief didn't know about the alien looking out the window (even though it was just a picture). He didn't know about the bed that made you feel like you were floating (even though it was just a water bed). Or the out-of-this-galaxy food (even though it was just regular food). When someone hasn't been somewhere that you have, it's like you're going for the first time, too. I couldn't wait. Only this time when we packed I had to include the eight books.

After dinner, I took out my sketch pad with the sand castle. If I'd read those books I could have been building that castle. Now I wouldn't have time.

The next morning, we took off for Pensacola Beach. Before long, Chief parked in front of our alien getaway. "The Spaceship Reed has landed!" he announced.

"Watch out for the aliens!" Mom called.

"*We're* the aliens," I reminded her.

Tori rolled her eyes, though I could tell she was having fun, too. Because when Tori wasn't having fun, everyone heard about it.

I unpacked, then I put the leash on Bruna and we ran down the beach. The sand slowed her pace until we reached the wet part where the water licked the shore.

Chief set up the grill and barbecued moon-burgers that night. Sam decided she just wanted a Martian Delight, which was really a dill pickle sandwich. And we all ate a huge mound of Pluto Potatoes that tasted and looked a lot like French fries.

After dinner, Sam and Tori headed to the beach, but Mom made me stay inside to read. I looked at the tower of books. I didn't know where to begin, so I closed my eyes and shuffled them. Then I picked one.

Shiloh! I decided I might as well read the one that seemed the most interesting. And it was. It was the best book I'd ever read. Actually the only book I've ever really liked.

That night, when Mom turned out the lights, I wanted to keep reading. The next morning when I reached the last few pages, a big lump crowded my throat. And when I got to the very last page, I read it again because I didn't want the story to end. I stared at the ceiling awhile, then I looked at the remaining books. How could I pick from that pile when I'd finished a book like *Shiloh*?

But I didn't have to. At least not for now, because Mom said, "Why don't you take off the rest of the day? Go get some fresh air."

I grabbed my sketch pad, walked down to the beach, and joined my sisters.

"Want to build a sand castle?" I called out to them. When they reached me, I showed them my drawing.

"Wow!" Sam said.

Tori scowled. "How are we going to build that?"

"Together," I said.

To my surprise, Tori said, "Well, we better get moving. A castle like that could take all day."

Soon we were filling buckets of damp sand and stacking the sand piles together. We hardly said a word. We just walked back and forth to the water. By the time we started digging the moat, a small crowd of people came up and watched.

"That's a sharp-looking castle," one man said.

A lady who'd been watching and chatting with us for about twenty minutes told the man, "They're sisters."

The man nodded, rubbing his chin. "Talent must run in their family."

People watched us for a while, then they walked away and another group made their way over to us. One thing was for sure, no one passed by without stopping. Finally the two people I wanted the most to see our masterpiece came out of the spaceship and joined us.

Chief whistled. "Now that's what I call a castle!"

"How did you ever plan such a thing?" Mom asked.

"Piper designed it," Tori said. And the way

she said those words made me think she wasn't embarrassed that I was her sister and had read only one book all summer.

Mom studied my drawing. "Piper, you really are a talented artist."

I looked up at her and winked. "I guess I take after Coco Kappel."

The five of us settled next to the castle and waited for the tide to come in and fill the moat. When it did, Tori took a picture with her camera.

"You should make a painting of it," I told Mom.

"No, Piper," she said. "*You* should."

Maybe I would. I could do anything when I set my mind to it. I could teach Bruna tricks, finish reading a good book, and design a spectacular castle.

The sun started to set and Chief mentioned that we should clean up and go to my favorite restaurant on the beach. The one he and I had visited a few nights before he shipped out.

"Get off the bus!" I yelled. Then I grew quiet and said, "Can we do something first?"

"What did you have in mind?" Mom asked.

"Yeah," said Tori, who suddenly sounded grumpy. "It won't take long, will it? I'm hungry."

"Only a moment," I said.

And a moment later the five of us were lined up in the sand, flat on our backs with our arms stretched out, making long strokes. Then, Bruna pranced around us, barking, creating

sandflakes with her paw prints. It was just like before. Only this time it was better. Because this time Chief was there, too.

On the way to the restaurant, Sam said, "Let's sing songs."

"Okay," Mom said. "Any suggestions?"

"I have one," I said. "It goes: A pimple on the nose, a pimple on the nose—"

My entire family hollered, "Piper Reed!"

"Just kidding," I said. "I meant the farmer in the dell, the farmer in the dell . . ."

While we drove to the restaurant, I decided I'd changed my mind about home. Home was not Pensacola, San Diego, Guam, or any of the other places we might have lived. In fact, home wasn't any particular place at all. Home was my family. Even if they didn't get my jokes sometimes.

GOFISH

QUESTIONS FOR THE AUTHOR

KIMBERLY WILLIS HOLT

What did you want to be when you grew up?
A writer.

When did you realize you wanted to be a writer?
In seventh grade, three teachers encouraged my writing. That was when I first thought the dream could come true. Before that, I didn't think I could be a writer because I wasn't a great student and I read slowly.

What's your first childhood memory?
Buying an orange Dreamsicle from the ice-cream man. I was two years old.

What's your most embarrassing childhood memory?
In fourth grade, I tried to impress the popular girls that I wanted to be friends with by doing somersaults in front of them. (I never learned to do cartwheels.) They called me a showoff, so I guess it didn't work. If only I'd known how to do a cartwheel.

What was your worst subject in school?
Algebra.

What was your first job?
I was in the movies. I popped popcorn at the Westside Cinemas.

How did you celebrate publishing your first book?
I'm sure my family went out to dinner. We always celebrate by eating.

Where do you write your books?
I write several places—a soft, big chair in my bedroom, at a table on my screen porch, or at coffee shops.

Where do you find inspiration for your writing?
Most of the inspiration for my writing comes from moments in my childhood.

Which of your characters is most like you?
I'm a bit like most of them. However, I fashioned Tori in the Piper Reed books after me. But Tori is bossier than I was and she certainly makes better grades than I did.

When you finish a book, who reads it first?
My daughter listens to me read my first draft.

Are you a morning person or a night owl?
I'm a morning person.

What's your idea of the best meal ever?
That's a toss-up. My grandmother's chicken and dumplings, and sushi.

Which do you like better: cats or dogs?
I'm a dog person. I have a poodle named Bronte who is the model for Bruna.

What do you value most in your friends?
Loyalty and honesty.

Where do you go for peace and quiet?
Home.

Who is your favorite fictional character?
Leroy in *Mister and Me* because he is forgiving. And that's a trait many of us don't have.

What are you most afraid of?
Anything harming my daughter.

What time of the year do you like best?
Fall.

What is your favorite TV show?
CBS Sunday Morning.

If you were stranded on a desert island, who would you want for company?
My husband and daughter.

What's the best advice you have ever received about writing?
A writer once told me, "Readers either see what they read or hear what they read. Writers have to learn to write for both." When I started following that advice, my writing improved.

What do you want readers to remember about your books?
The characters. I want them to seem like real people. I want them to miss them and wonder what happened to them.

What would you do if you ever stopped writing?
I plan on dying with a pen in my hand.

What do you like best about yourself?
I'm honest.

What is your worst habit?
I eat too much.

What do you consider to be your greatest accomplishment?
I gave birth to a wonderful human being.

What do you wish you could do better?
I wish I could do a cartwheel.

What would your readers be most surprised to learn about you?
I send gift cards with positive messages to myself when I order something for me.

*K*eep reading for an excerpt from
Piper Reed Gets a Job,
available in hardcover from Henry Holt.

EXCERPT

Beep, beep. Six thirty. I turned off the alarm, threw off my covers, and popped out of bed. My insides did flip-flops. There was something exciting about the first day of school. Especially when it was everybody's first day of school. Not like last year, when we moved to Pensacola in October and I was the only new kid in class. This year, the first day of school meant new notebooks, new pencils, new shoes, new teacher, and a new seat at the back of the class. Everything would be new except for me.

I wondered if Mr. Clark would be my teacher this year. He gave out treat coupons when students got the correct answers. Or maybe I'd be assigned to Mrs. Lindsey. She designed the butterfly garden outside the fifth-grade wing. Her students got extra time outside to take care of the garden.

Instead of sitting in the front of the class like my teacher, Ms. Gordon, made me do last year, I planned to pick a seat at the back near the window. That way I could watch butterflies dart around the salvia in the garden. It was going to be a get-off-the-bus kind of year.

Then I walked inside the school and everything changed. The school secretary grinned at me from behind the registration table.

"Good morning, Piper Reed! How was your summer?"

"How did you know my name?" I asked her. There were hundreds of kids at our school.

"Piper Reed, everyone knows your name. You're famous at Blue Angels Elementary School." She handed me a piece of paper. "Here's your room assignment."

Room 308.

"There must be a mistake—308 was my room last year," I said.

She shook her head. "There's no mistake. We have more fifth-graders this year, so we had to put one class in the fourth-grade hall."

Getting room 308, again, meant I'd have to change my plans. I wouldn't be able to see the butterfly garden. Then I remembered the tree outside the window. Instead of watching butterflies, I'd watch squirrels and birds.

On the way to class, I ran into Michael and Nicole. Michael didn't look happy either. "Room 308 again. Boring!"

"I'm in room 405," said Nicole as she headed toward the *real* fifth-grade hall.

Michael and I walked into 308 together. It even smelled the same—old paste mixed with stinky sneakers. We rushed to the back of the room and chose seats in the row nearest the window. Outside, a cardinal landed on a branch of the huge tree. Watching birds wasn't like watching butterflies, but it was better than the blackboard.

A moment later, Ms. Gordon walked in. How could a teacher forget it was the first day of school? Maybe she forgot something in her old desk drawer.

"Sorry, Michael and Piper," she said, "but that's not going to work. You two need to take your former seats, where I can keep an eye on you."

I stayed seated. "Ms. Gordon, this is a *fifth*-grade class now."

Just then, Hailey entered the classroom, followed by show-off-know-it-all Kami.

"Hi, Ms. Gordon," Kami said, prancing to the same seat where she sat last year. "I'm so glad you're our teacher again."

I picked up my new notebooks and new pencil case and walked to my old desk. The first day of school loses all its specialness when you get last year's teacher and have to sit in your same old seat in the same old classroom.

That first week dragged like an ant climbing Mount Everest. We reviewed fractions, learned how to write in different tenses, and studied our vocabulary lists. It was exactly like last year, only Nicole wasn't there. Lucky Nicole got Mrs. Lindsey and had already started working in the butterfly garden.

"We planted purple coneflowers today," she told me. "They attract the Viceroy butterfly."

Finally Saturday arrived. The Gypsy Club was due at my house any minute. Paint fumes filled the living room. Mom was busy painting the backdrop for my big sister, Tori's, middle school play. Her drama coach asked Mom to create it since she was the art teacher at the elementary school. She'd set up a makeshift table out of plywood and two sawhorses. It ran the entire length of the living room, leaving no space for the Gypsy Club. We'd have to find a new place to meet.

Last year, when I was in fourth grade, Mom substituted for our art teacher who was on maternity leave. Now Mrs. Kimmel wanted to stay home with her baby. So Mom got to be the art teacher officially. At first I thought it would be cool having Mom as a teacher, but I soon learned there weren't any benefits. She never said my art projects were the best, even if they were.

My little sister, Sam, was probably the only one who got special treatment because she was six and the baby of the family. My parents thought everything Sam did was spectacular. They practically broke into applause whenever she remembered to feed her goldfish, Peaches the Second.

While I tried to figure out where to hold the meeting, the doorbell rang. I answered the door and found the other three Gypsy Club members—Michael, Nicole, and Hailey.

"Follow me," I told them. We had no choice but to go to my room—the room I shared with Sam. This afternoon, she'd posted a sign on the door that read QUIET! WRITER AT WORK!

Inside the room, Sam sat cross-legged on the bed with a thick tablet on her lap. She was probably writing another princess story. That's what spelling bee prodigies do in their spare time. They weren't like normal six-year-old kids who ride bikes and play hide-and-seek. Spelling bee prodigies read and write for fun. Tori wasn't a prodigy, but she liked reading and writing, too. Chief said someone had to break the mold. I guess I was the mold breaker because I hated to read and write.

When we entered the room, Sam frowned. "Hey! I'm busy writing."

Hailey plopped on to Sam's bed.

"I have to have my Gypsy Club meeting here," I told her. "Mom's backdrop is swallowing the living room."

"Well," said Sam, "if you're going to have the meeting here, then I get to be in the Gypsy Club." She was always trying to weasel her way in.

"No way," I told her. "Besides it's my room, too."

Sam glared at Hailey and Nicole. "Then Gypsy Club members aren't allowed on *my* side of the room."

Hailey bounced up from Sam's bed and switched to mine. But Nicole stayed seated. "I love stories," she told Sam. "What is yours about?"

Sam smiled, probably thrilled to have an admirer. "A princess."

"Nicole," I said, "come over on my side. We need to start the meeting."

Nicole slowly inched over the invisible line that now divided our room.

I stood at attention. "Everyone stand so that we can say the Gypsy Club creed."

Together we recited the words that began each meeting. The creed reminded us that we were Navy brats, moving every couple of years or sometimes sooner.

"We are the Gypsies of land and sea. We——"

In a loud voice, Sam said, "Once upon a time . . ."

We ignored her, raising our voices. "We travel from port to port——"

Sam continued, "there lived a beautiful princess in a beautiful castle who had to share a room with her mean, ugly sister."

Nicole stopped and turned toward Sam, but the rest of us kept reciting. "And everywhere we go, we let people know——"

Sam shouted, "Everyone loved the beautiful princess, but no one liked the mean, ugly sister who wouldn't let the beautiful princess be in her club." She stretched out on her stomach.

"Okay," I said, "let's get out of here."

"Great idea!" said Michael.

"Stupendous idea!" said Hailey.

"But I want to hear the rest of Sam's story," said Nicole, looking longingly toward Sam.

Sam stared up from her page. "You can stay."

I grabbed Nicole's hand and led the Gypsy Club out of my room and into Tori's. We'd be safe there since Tori went with her friends to the base movie. At least I thought we'd be safe until the lumpy tower of clothes in the corner started to move toward us.

Hailey gasped.

"What's that?" Nicole yelled.

We froze, waiting for a giant rat to emerge from the pile. Instead our dog, Bruna, popped out from under the blue jeans, T-shirts, and shorts.

"Oh, it's just Bruna," Michael said, but I heard the relief in his voice.

Bruna wagged her tail and went over to each of us, waiting for a pat on the head.

We stepped over the shoes with pointy heels scattered on the floor until we got to a clear spot. Movie star posters covered her wall along with one that said EMILY DICKINSON IS COOL. A framed picture of Ronnie Cartwright was on her nightstand. He didn't give it to Tori. She'd found skateboard boy's image on a Web site and printed it out.

I cleared my throat. "Now as I was trying to say, Halloween is around the corner and—"

"GET OUT OF MY ROOM!" Tori yelled from the doorway. The movie must have ended early. Her face was red. Her eyes bulged. Her hands curled into fists at her sides.

Nicole took off. She rushed past Tori and down the hall. We heard her feet thump down the steps and the front door squeak open and slam shut.

As Hailey and Michael eased backward out of Tori's room, I tried to explain. "We had no choice."

Tori's hands flew to her hips. "There are always choices. And sneaking into my room is not one of them." She pointed toward the door.

A moment later, Hailey, Michael, and I joined Nicole outside. Nicole wrapped her arms around her body like a ball of tightly wound string. "Your sister is scary."

"Both of my sisters are scary," I said. "They're aliens from Jupiter."

I missed my tree house in San Diego where I could escape Tori and Sam. But after Chief got assigned to NAS Pensacola, Florida, we moved into military housing. Now we lived in a small townhouse with a tiny yard and one puny tree. There was hardly enough room for Bruna to run around.

"We need another meeting place," Hailey muttered. "We could meet at our house, but I have a pesky little brother."

Michael dug in his pocket and pulled out a folded magazine picture. "I have an idea. I was going to show this later, but now is the perfect time."

We watched him slowly unfold the picture until it revealed a clubhouse with a window box and wood shingle roof.

"Get off the bus!" we hollered.

Just then thunder rumbled and a raindrop landed on the tip of my nose. A few seconds later, it began to sprinkle. Then, as if someone flipped a switch, the sprinkle turned into a downpour.

When we dashed inside the townhouse, I accidentally knocked over a can of paint next to the sawhorse. Periwinkle poured out onto the drop cloth, forming a puddle.

"Piper!" Mom yelled.

We needed that clubhouse quick.